A Speci...
Hardback ...

limited to just 70 numbered co...

Ida Keogh

Ida Keogh

This is number: 48

FISH!

NP Novellas:

Ida Keogh

NewCon Press
England

First published in the UK December 2021 by
NewCon Press
41 Wheatsheaf Road,
Alconbury Weston,
Cambs, PE28 4LF

NPN013 (limited edition hardback)
NPN014 (paperback)

10 9 8 7 6 5 4 3 2 1

ISBN:

978-1-914953-06-4 (hardback)
978-1-914953-07-1 (paperback)

Cover layout and design by Ian Whates

Typesetting and editorial meddling by Ian Whates
Text layout by Ian Whates

The Reporter

I thought when I hit the water it would be warm, welcoming, its waves parting for me like a lover's thighs. I felt delirious from the evening's cocktail of Prosecco and ketamine, the latter urged upon me by the captain himself in front of the others, no doubt as some form of insurance policy to stop me naming him in my piece. In the mauve and ochre sunset, the higher I climbed up the yacht's rigging the gentler the waves seemed, like ripples on a pond caressed by a fall of cherry blossom. It invited me to plunge deep into its liquid embrace and float, insensate and at peace.

But the ocean is a treacherous bitch. The shock of the water slamming against my body made me gasp, then sent my teeth cracking together as my head snapped back, striking the surface with such force I blacked out for a moment. Certainly, my next recollection was that I was sinking, a sharp stab of saltwater flooding my nose, my mouth and my lungs.

In the panic, flailing limbs became tangled in the silk of my long summer dress; a blur of red surrounded me. I felt my right shoe slip off, and for a perverse moment wondered how I had climbed the rigging wearing Louboutins. I imagined a champagne flute tumbling after me, showering the deck with an arc of effervescent pink spray, smashing against the rail and plunging down through the swell like a knife.

I twisted in the water. Above me, the underside of the ocean's surface undulated and churned: one moment a blaze of fire, the next a whorled ceiling of mercury. The yacht's keel cut across it, a dark tear which seemed to shrink and repair itself as I sank.

I must have passed out again, because when my eyes re-focused I was looking down toward the ocean floor. My mind reeled. The bleached bones of a whale reached up to me, a God-like hand emerging from the sand to bring me home. A shoal of fish glittered between those pale monoliths, neon purple and gold. Impulsively, I tried to breathe. A string of bubbles floated up from my mouth, crystal balls telling impossibly small fortunes. In that instant, suspended in the darkening water, I believed there was only one fate awaiting me: bone fingers closing around my flesh as I sank into the hungry sand.

The rest is a haze. I remember a sound, like tinnitus, quiet and piercing. An unexpected breath, at first sweet and shallow then deeper, filling my lungs with hope. Lips against mine. Soft, cold.

I woke on the beach, caressed by the susurration of midnight waves. Hair slicked my face, encrusted with sand and salt. A sine wave of phosphorescent blue stretched away along the shore. I watched for a moment as it encroached and retreated, encroached and retreated: nature's heartbeat glowing there before me in the biological jetsam, reminding me I was alive.

My dress was a ruin. Its remnants clung to my waist and legs. My breasts were pressed into the fine, cool grit, my back exposed to the night breeze.

You see these films where the victims of pirates wash up on baking sand, always under a glaring sun turning parched lips to craquelure, retching salt water, hands clawing to pull themselves from the sea. It wasn't like that.

I was calm. I felt a little light-headed, but my breath rose and fell evenly along with the gentle tide. My skin tingled.

I sat up slowly, brushed damp grains from my skin. I tugged at my dress until the fabric gave way, and tore off a long strip to tie around my chest. I stood, wavering slightly. Surf sucked at my toes. I shrugged at the loss of my other shoe.

I couldn't see the yacht, or anyone on the beach.

Looking back, I wonder why I didn't scream for help, or run in a panic, or cry. Instead, I felt an overwhelming sense of gratitude that I could hear the ocean's pulse without interruption. I found myself humming a strange melody I wouldn't hear again until the refugees came with their songs and their battle scars.

I wandered aimlessly, and after a while I saw the lambent lights of the harbour casting twinkling pinpricks of colour onto the black water. I was strangely unmoved by the sight. Rather than relief, I felt a sense of loss.

An hour later I was back in my hotel room, where I rinsed the salt from my skin and sank into bed, still damp. I slept for two days.

My editor was furious, of course. All the footage had been left on the yacht. It was encrypted on my phone, so they wouldn't find out who I was, but the elaborate set up had been wasted. I was supposed to play the party girl but falling into the ocean and being presumed drowned until I called in two days later wasn't part of the plan.

The captain, who had been ready enough to take the bribe, was far more reticent when it came to explaining what had happened to me. On a crackling line, he told me the party had got out of hand, I had drunk too much, had too much K, as though he had given me a choice about that.

He told me the dreams weren't real, that I must have been hallucinating, that I was lucky to be alive and he wasn't going to take responsibility. But I knew. I knew every time I woke, comforted by the shred of memory. Her soft lips on mine. Pale satin hands, three-fingered and webbed with translucent skin, sharp nails ripping open my dress to allow me to breathe her in. Her touch on my spine, electric, thrilling. The hum of her song vibrating through me with shudders of pleasure.

I knew it was her as soon as I saw her on the news footage, palms spread on the other side of green-tinged glass, her eyes wide with fear, her silvered tail thrashing.

Now it was my turn to save her.

The Deserter

Found. Captured, I, netted. Afraid. Placed where brine ends on all sides, like surface, tipped wrong. Hard as rock slab. Creatures move all around. Move like upright blue lobsters with short, white tails. Make sounds so slow. Vibrations in air. Air they need. I know this. I have seen.

Gave breath to one, two.

One many tides ago. Beautiful tail, not its own. Red like blood. Wrapped around blue skin, wrapped around bones. No scales. Red tail tore at my touch. Not its own. It twitched like injured long-fish. Blue skin warm. I sang to it. Tried to warn it. They were coming. It did not understand. It convulsed. Wrapped around me. Held it, I. Sang of war. Sang of swimming away. Abandoning clan. Finding safety. Gave it breath again. It tried to sing, low moan like child. Entered my mouth with slick tongue, like in union. It sang higher. Reminiscent of love song. Sad, I, to think of love then. Both singing, not same language. Sad it did not understand.

A few tides past, I gave breath to another, made of bones wrapped in dark skin. No fins. No red tail. Not the same. It floated, then sank. It did not sing. Bore the mark of the clan's flick stinger. Blood in deep water. Let it sink. Too late for air. It could not sing. Maybe taken by teeth-beasts. Could not stop to see. They were coming.

No choice, I. Swam to shallows. Forbidden. Waited for sunlight piercing turquoise. Many creatures came. Sang to all of war. They tried to sing in air, shrill like eel. Reminiscent of fear. Four came with net. None had tails. None sang of love.

Air I can breathe. Water I prefer. Air is forbidden, like shallows. Brine-cage is warm. Too much salt. Every day it is new water. At least clean. They bring me whole fish, alive, as if I am teeth-beast. I kill fish by hitting it against brine cage but have to rip with my teeth. Not good fish. Shallow fish.

Sometimes the creatures try to sing. Strange harmonies. Sometimes regular like crab claw clicks. Once, song of blue great-one. Surprised, I, they can sing like blue great-one. I dance. Creatures watch. Then sing like squeaker-fish. Like round-fish. Like teeth-beast. Frustrated, I. Know all these songs, but not my language. I become male. Beat my tail against the brine-cage. Scream war cry. Maybe that they understand. Creatures are silent then for many waves.

One day they sing like me. My voice. Sing my own voice to me. Mouths don't move. I sing back, to ghost of myself. I think they want to sing to me. I point all around. Sing the

11

name of water. I point to my body. Sing the name of tail, scales, hands, face, teeth. They sing back to me. They point to their hands, though they have too many fingers. They point to their mouths, their eyes, their hair. Bring me fish. I sing name of fish. They hold up one, two. Sing name of fish back. They learn. I dance for them. They point to things they move on. I have no word, so sing the name for crab legs. They make gestures with their hands, hitting palms together. Such a noise, even in air. I make gesture back to them, like they sing back to me.

Soon when they sing back they make other gestures with hands. Small shapes I copy. When they have a name I do not know, they show me shapes for it. I learn the shapes. They call themselves man. They call me Larimar. It is stone they tell me, blue like the ocean. Hard and beautiful.

One day I ask for no more shallow fish. Instead round fish. Crab. Teeth-beast. They dance for me. They bring me a feast.

I don't eat. Make sign for blade. Will not eat like teeth-beast any more. They put heads towards heads, make quiet sounds in air. They bring me small blade. Not shell. Shiny like sunlight on waves. Man substance. I know this. I have seen. Dangerous, but allows me to gut round fish. To hollow crab. I gorge. In slab of teeth-beast I carve for them the ritual form for peace. Offer to them. Men are silent again for many waves.

They bring more people. Different colours. They sign, they sing. They tell me more like me are coming. Tell them, I. Scream. Not like me. They are coming, and they will kill. Men say they are safe on land, but I know they need the water too. They do not know what I know. Clan's flick stingers will seem like tiny child of jellyfish.

Many tides later red tail comes to me. I know it, though it has changed colour. Now it is silver tail. I make silver tail for it. Its eyes make water. Presses against brine cage. Signs it has seen pictures of me. Pictures I know. They show me pictures of so many fish, of coral, of ruined man carriers, asking where to find the clan. Some pictures I know. Some I do not. Ocean is large, and I cannot tell them the way.

Red now silver tail signs it will make me free. I dance for it. They take its tail. Give it man substance like shell on its back, covered in tubes. It comes into the brine cage. I see bubbles. Tubes give air. Air it doesn't need when I am here. I pull the tubes away. Give air to silver tail. It sings again, sings like love. Clings to me with its many fingered hands. I dance with it. I sing of freedom.

Many tides later, I sing of love.

The Whistle Blower

"Their skin works in the same way as an octopus."

"You think this thing is related to octopuses?"

"Octopodes."

"What?"

"The plural. It's octopodes. And no, they're not related. A lot of species use chromatophores to change colour." Zara scribbled another note, then clipped her pen to the board. "Will this take long? It's just I have hours of observation yet and then I have to type all this up."

"This is important Miss Flores. We take national security very seriously."

"Doctor. I have a doctorate in marine biology."

"Well, then. Dr Flores. I just want to know, can it camouflage itself as anything?"

"He, not it. He's currently in a male state. We are still experimenting, but so far he has shown a profound aptitude for natural background replication. Rocks, coral, even moving plant life. We have tried artificial backgrounds but the results are varied. I think some patterns are learned.

There's technically no reason why he shouldn't be able to replicate any background, though. The chromatophores are highly advanced organs in the skin. The pigment sacs are extremely fine and can produce a full range of colours, even some beyond our visible spectrum. They are activated neurally but we're still not sure whether the colours are instinctive or a matter of choice. If it's the latter, there ought to be no limitation on the available patterns."

The General tapped at the glass. "How long does it take?"

"For the chromatophores to work? Milliseconds."

"So, what are these colours we're seeing now? It's asleep isn't it?"

"He is asleep. I think he's dreaming."

"Does the skin still work when you remove it?"

Zara's mouth dropped open. She glared at him. "We only have three merfolk in this facility, General. They are all healthy adults and as far as we can tell, highly intelligent. Dissection is absolutely out of the question. In any event, it wouldn't work. As I said, the chromatophores are neurally stimulated. No brain, no pretty colours. The same as an octopus. There are plenty of them you can experiment on if you so choose."

"Do we need three, though? I remember my biology classes Dr Flores, you can learn a lot cutting things open."

"You can also learn a lot through communication. We are working on a signing system with Larimar, that's what we've called our subject number two. We already have a clear understanding of the internal biology from MRI scanning, and we have multiple skin samples which have been extensively tested. I appreciate your interest in them, but their health and well-being are my absolute priority."

"We'll see, Dr Flores. Remember who pays for this facility. I outrank you here. Now, tell me about the pheromones."

Zara sighed. She had already compiled a complete briefing on this. "What do you want to know, General?"

"Can they be harvested? Can we use them?"

Zara's brow furrowed. "You want to militarise them?"

"No need to concern yourself with the wider applications, Dr Flores. Can it be done?"

"I assume you're talking about the female pheromones. When in the female state merfolk produce small quantities of pheromones which are released through the skin, primarily through glands in the neck and wrists. The effect is a mild sexual stimulant on Merfolk in a male state, but it acts as a powerful intoxicant and aphrodisiac to humans. Any physical contact with Merfolk will induce strong arousal in both men and women."

"How long does it last?"

"It varies from individual to individual. So far all experiments have been aborted at an early stage."

"Why's that? You can't be short of willing volunteers?" He chuckled.

"Again, General, my priority is the health and well-being of the subjects. Exposing them to the further attentions of our divers would be highly inappropriate. But in any event, anyone who has been in the tanks with a subject in a female state so far has tried to remove their breathing apparatus to get closer to them."

"You mean they risk drowning?"

"In short, yes. As I said, it is highly intoxicating."

"Have you tried it?"

"No, and I don't intend to, thank you. I am here to observe, not to indulge."

"So can you extract it?"

"We took a selection of water samples which contained a dilute version. The pheromone dissipated quickly, though."

"And out of the water? Have you tried extraction when the subject is dry?"

"Secretion only happens in water."

"Here's where we come back to dissection Dr Flores. I'll bet you could suck those glands dry if we better utilised one of your subjects."

"You would kill an intelligent species just to harvest a small quantity of a sex drug? Are you kidding me?"

"No need to get upset, Dr Flores. I'm just thinking strategically. Whatever happens to your subjects from here on in is above your pay grade, do you understand?"

In one hand Zara clutched a whisky tumbler, a single ice cube slowly melting into her third serving. In the other she held the data stick, loaded with footage of Larimar from her first days in captivity to her signing and communicating with the science team, stills of the carvings she had produced and wav files of her singing. She waited nervously for the call. When her mobile rang she jumped, nearly spilling her drink.

"Dr Flores? I'm Ingrid Spearman. You say you have footage that might interest us?"

"Yes, like nothing you've seen before. But before I tell you about it, I need to make sure I will have absolute anonymity. You understand I'm breaching national security just by talking to you."

"Of course. We always protect our sources. What do you have for us?"

"I need to guarantee you will get this out. They're going to kill them. They're going to dissect the most important scientific discovery ever made."

"That depends on what you have for us. You're a marine biologist? Is this a giant octopus or something?"

"No, this is something far more important. Ms Spearman, we have mermaids."

The Police Sergeant

The files were stacked high when Constable Turner came in. It was late, getting on for 2am. There seemed to be no end to this shift. I took off my glasses and pinched my nose.

"What have you got for me, Turner?"

"Tip off, Sarge, from old Harry. You know, the sex offender?"

I knew old Harry. He had done a stint for kiddy porn back in the day and couldn't seem to keep himself off the register. These days he was a useful informant – gave us the heads up about new brothels, or old ones where things were getting out of hand. He swore he never looked at kids anymore and in exchange for his assistance we turned a blind eye to his own use of the local prostitutes.

"What's the news?" I said, though I wasn't sure I wanted to hear it.

"He says there's something weird going on down at the docks. Something new, got all his kinky friends excited. It's high class, too expensive for him. But one of his mates told him it was dangerous. Like, life and death dangerous."

"Who's running it?"

"New outfit. He doesn't know the boys on the door and they keep it locked tight. We've secured a warrant, but I think we'll need a full team down there if it's that out of the ordinary."

• "What, now?" I sighed. Suddenly the paperwork was looking good.

"It's like a pop-up, sir. Places like this don't stay around very long, they attract too much attention. They could move on any time."

I rubbed my eyes. "Sure, why not. We'll pretend I don't have better things to do than get my riot gear on and go chasing a bunch of hookers."

The docks were grim at night. We drove in a van with two unmarked cars as escort. Shipping containers towered above us, casting everything in shadow. We found the place, an old warehouse with faded signs and concrete walls crumbling from sea salt. A single street lamp lit the door up a sickly yellow. There were two men outside, both of whom looked like they could happily take on a wrestling team. We parked up a little way back and got ready to burst from the van.

When we did, one of the two bruisers scarpered. The other banged on the door, then ducked inside.

"Police! Open up!" I shouted. They did not open up, and the door remained firmly locked. We got into position to breach. I beckoned forward Constable Pearce who had the hydraulic breaker. It let out a loud *whump* and the door swung open.

Inside it was dark and smelled of damp. Someone found a light switch and two strip lights blinked into life, exposing a small room with a desk and a few chairs. I could hear music coming from a door at the back. I had a call on my radio – one of the team had found the back door, left wide open. I sent them off with a brief description of our two thugs. We moved to the back of the room. The door was locked, so we got the breaker out again.

Behind the door lay the warehouse proper. A large disco ball hung from the ceiling, providing the only light: a hundred little circles, slowly spinning. It took me a while to work out what I was seeing. The room was full of tanks. Big, glass tanks. I switched on my torch and shone it around. I counted five of the things, all in a line. I walked over to the closest. My foot crunched on something. I looked down and saw a pile of fish bones. My torchlight caught something else and I kept it on the floor so I didn't trip over. It looked like a body. I slowly moved the beam up and down. Not a body. A wet suit. Next to it was a pile of scuba gear. It lay in a tangled heap, hurriedly abandoned. Water pooled around it. There was a ladder on the side of the tank. Someone had been for a dip. I scratched my head. Where were all the girls?

I shone my torch at the tank but all I could see was dirty water. Then it moved. The water swirled in front of me and

I caught a flash of something. Someone was still in there. "Turner! Styles!" I shouted. "Get your lights on this tank. I think we've got one. They'll have to come up for air sometime soon."

Turner saw it first. When she shone her torch at the tank something hit the glass on the other side. It looked like a woman, but she didn't have any scuba gear on. My first thought was that she would be drowning in there and I was about to throw off my shoes and jump in the tank. But then we all saw it. She didn't have legs. She had a tail. We'd seen the footage but nobody believed it. We thought it was a hoax. But here she was, a real life fucking mermaid.

We found the owner of the scuba gear naked and hiding in a cupboard. He was just a customer, he said. Paid five grand for a chance to dive with a mermaid. One touch and you're in heaven. We could all see that; he couldn't hide his embarrassment. I threw him some overalls I found in the corner. After he'd calmed down he was more cooperative. Gave us good descriptions of the woman on the desk and the guy he'd given the money to. We weren't sure what to charge him with so we let him go.

I called it in, and about an hour later the whole place was crawling with government agents trying to make us all sign non-disclosure agreements. I had a feeling this wouldn't be the last we would see of these creatures, though. Even if only five had been caught and those by sex traffickers... How many more were out there?

The General

Operation Wavecrest: Briefing Update
Author: General **[REDACTED]**
Classification: Top Secret

Background:

Operation Wavecrest is the joint venture between the British Army and Royal Navy in response to the ongoing international Merfolk crisis. Coordinating at a high level with United States forces the primary aim of the operation is to monitor the newly discovered Merfolk species and to ensure the safety of UK, US and international waters. The second stage of the operation, for which I am responsible, is to ensure the safety of the UK mainland should the emerging refugee crisis continue as expected.

From October to December 2021, US forces apprehended five Merfolk from locations around the Gulf of Mexico. The Royal Navy was appraised and three of the subjects were transferred into UK custody for specialist surveillance and testing.

On 10 March 2022, the Trafalgar Class attack submarine HMS Goldwing entered international waters and proceeded to the Puerto Rico trench south of the Virgin Islands, where US forces indicated sightings of Merfolk had been focussed. A six-man bathyscaphe was deployed and footage relayed. This gave the crew of HMS Goldwing real time images of the trench. The bathyscaphe descended to a depth of approximately 2,000 metres, nearly a quarter of the depth of the trench, before unusual sonar was picked up. The bathyscaphe found a plateau approximately 2 kilometres wide adjacent to a series of cave structures on the eastern side of the trench. Both visual and infrared scans were activated.

The footage obtained from this descent gave cause for alarm. The bathyscaphe had descended directly into the centre of a conflict between Merfolk tribes, namely those inhabiting the caves and an invasive force on the plateau. The scene is not easily forgotten. Ranks of armed Merfolk lined the plateau. The front line rode on sharks, which were crudely armoured. Of greatest concern, a form of trebuchet was positioned centrally and loaded with a boulder of significant size. A blue whale was seen nearby, harnessed with some form of thick rope. This was presumably how the trebuchet had been erected. The last footage from the bathyscaphe showed the trebuchet being fired in its direction. Despite attempting evasive manoeuvres, the bathyscaphe suffered a direct hit. The resulting explosion killed all six crew. The bathyscaphe was unrecoverable. HMS Goldwing took the decision to report rather than to deploy a further bathyscaphe or to intervene in the warfare. In its retreat, HMS Goldwing's sonar detected large numbers of fish fleeing the area. Given the depth at which these fish were detected it is now suspected these were in fact Merfolk. The direction of travel indicates an exodus moving easterly into the Atlantic.

In the following months reports emerged of Merfolk sightings around the UK coastline. Leaks were initially contained to the conspiracy press, but it became clear a response would be required as the problem grew in scale. On 6 May 2022 footage was leaked from the UK's Merfolk observation facility. This was widely dismissed as a hoax, however, this breach in national security could not be contained and led rapidly to international interest in the subject.

On 14 September 2022 the private Hergowitz expedition set out to explore the Puerto Rico trench region. Franz Hergowitz used four bathyscaphes, covering a significant area of the trench at depths as low as 3,000 metres. The footage obtained from the expedition was published online and quickly went viral. Merfolk were now impossible to deny and were firmly under the public gaze.

In the meantime, sightings have increased along the UK coastline.

Progress report:

At its six month mark, the second stage of Operation Wavecrest is progressing as planned. Three coastal sites have been designated as refugee camps for the steadily growing influx of Merfolk. The Royal Navy and where appropriate the Coastguard will be deployed to seek out and capture as many Merfolk as possible and to transport them to the new sites. These areas will be fenced from the sea floor to the surface for containment. Measured quantities of fish will be transported daily to feed the Merfolk population. They can also consume kelp and other varieties of seaweed. Sites have been chosen specifically for their abundance of plant life. Merfolk will be allowed to keep belongings, but all weaponry shall be removed. We cannot risk different tribal factions continuing their war in our waters.

After containment comes re-education. Successful attempts were made with the Merfolk originally captured to evolve a three-fingered version of British Sign Language. Now their release has been agreed the project has been halted, however the learning techniques developed by lead scientist Dr Flores are transferable. Merfolk are a highly intelligent species and it is hoped they will learn quickly and pass on their understanding. Once a universal form of communication is established then re-education can commence.

The eventual goal will be re-colonisation of the Merfolk in international waters. Established communities under the protection and control of the international community and in self-sustaining environments will be the only way in the long term to preserve our fish stocks and to ensure peace.

In the meantime, all efforts must be made to prevent the full integration of Merfolk into British mainland society. Projections suggest that the cost of doing so would be prohibitive. Fresh infrastructure would be required, including saltwater canal systems and the re-purpose of existing buildings in large numbers to accommodate aquatic environments.

In short, if the number of refugees continues to increase the efforts to establish international colonies must be doubled. If such colonies cannot be negotiated then in lieu it will be necessary to establish quotas with other European countries who have been less affected by the crisis to ensure that they take their fair share of Merfolk. The potential impact on the British culture and way of life cannot be underestimated. The influx of foreign, indeed almost alien elements must be contained.

Both naval forces and ground troops will be held in a state of readiness and will not hesitate to engage should it prove necessary.

The Social Worker

The boat cast off with the creak of wood and the slap of water. Jacqui stood by the rail, watching seagulls swoop and call. She pulled her cardigan tight against the sudden breeze. The motor was a comforting hum beneath her feet as the boat chugged out of Portland Harbour. It turned east to circle the island. Jacqui stayed where she was on the port side, staring out at the grey sea, until the boat picked up speed beyond the harbour wall and the chill brought her out in goosebumps. She turned and descended metal steps to the lower deck and went inside. The air was musty. The summer passengers were all gone but they had left the lingering scent of sweat, sun cream and burgers from the little cafe bar which was now closed for the season. In the middle of the cabin was another flight of stairs, and she followed these down to the hull.

It was called a glass-bottomed boat, but it wasn't really; only the sides of the hull were thick plated glass and not the floor. A shame, she thought. Still the view was clear enough as they rounded the Bill. In contrast to the grey surface everything below was picked out in shades of yellow and green. Jacqui found a seat and gazed down on a jumble of rocks interspersed with beds of seaweed and stretches of softly undulating sand. A half-hidden lobster waved lazy antennae at her. A group of brown and cream wrasse swam by. There was more marine life than she had expected to see down here.

The boat juddered to a halt as it came to the entrance of the Sanctuary. From the prow Jacqui could see the enormous metal chain link fence which stretched from the sea floor up to the choppy surface, carving out eight cubic miles of water a short distance from Chesil Beach. An entrance gate slid back, metal clanking even through the thickness of the glass. Jacqui realised she was pressing her face to the window like a child in an aquarium. She took a step back, suddenly embarrassed. She did not have to wait for long. Soon faces appeared on the other side, looking in.

They crowded against the glass, flashing an array of colours over their skins. Tails thrashed and arms pushed as they jockeyed for position. Jacqui tried to remember her training modules. They're just as curious as I am, she thought. She stood near the glass and signed. *I am here to see Tomasin.* One of the Merfolk signed back that he would fetch them. Jacqui opened her tablet. She had photographs of Tomasin as both male and female for recognition. In either gender there could be no mistaking the ritual scarification across their chest. It was a beautiful design of whorls and dots, but Jacqui still shuddered inwardly with faint disgust at the thought of the Merfolk cutting into their own skin.

Tomasin was male today. Jacqui made a sign of greeting, which they returned. They then appeared to vocalise something to the surrounding Merfolk, who peeled off one by one, leaving them alone. She clicked to record video and began the interview.

Her palms sweated slightly as she signed. She learned that Tomasin had no family left. Were they prepared to leave their friends behind? How would they cope living with a different species? Jacqui knew her assessment would not only affect the rest of Tomasin's life, but could seal the fate of hundreds more Merfolk. If she gave the go ahead, Tomasin would be the first Merfolk to be taken in by a human family in the UK, though no doubt more would follow.

Tomasin had taken well to signing. They were calm as they communicated, their three-fingered hands moving smoothly through the water.

I will miss them, but not this place. I cannot be alone here. It is only water and sand and small rocks. There are no caves, and not enough distance to find my own space. Most folk don't mind, but I like to be alone. I wish to be beyond the fence, but we are forbidden. Why not try something else? Man will give me new home. Feed me. I will make art for them. Here not even allowed a stone knife. How can I carve? I will die here. Friends will all die here. We escape war and we are caged like beasts. We cannot live like this.

Jacqui had already vetted the Morgenstern family who had offered to sponsor Tomasin. He was a banker; she an art dealer. Their expansive swimming pool had been converted to salt water, and Jacqui had spoken to the aquarium specialist who had prattled on about live rocks and protein skimmers and algae scrubbing. Tomasin would swap one cage for another. If she signed off, they would effectively be living in indentured servitude, creating art for a bespoke audience who would no doubt make a significant profit. But what happened if she didn't? More refugees were turning up daily. It was ludicrously expensive to fence off areas of the coastline to make refugee camps, and the quality of life there was obviously poor. Wouldn't it be better if Merfolk could be contributing members of society?

Tomasin reached into a pouch strung around their waist. They pulled out a small figurine and held it up to the glass for Jacqui to see. Carved from a green, translucent stone, it was roughly globe shaped, and spirals and tentacles coiled delicately around the entire piece. It reminded her of a sleeping octopus, or a nest of eels. She stared at it, taking in its strange beauty until Tomasin returned it to the pouch. *This is what I live for. Let me create. Let me live.*

Jacqui returned to the railings for the return journey, enjoying the gusts of salt spray. By the time the boat pulled back into the harbour, she knew what her recommendation would be.

The Makeup Artist

First, you apply shadow to the lids. I like to go for these plum and scarlet shades by Creative. Totally warlike, they make you feel ready to fight, you know? They glide on super easy, though obviously you would use a good primer first. Get the purple deep into the crease, then the red on the lid itself. Don't worry if it looks really intense and angry right at the start, we're going to blend it with some other amazing products.

Fuck, this is so bizarre. Fucking warrior mermaids actually exist. But whatever, they don't wear makeup, they live underwater. Salt water. It's the worst for primer.

Okay, so now we're ready for some shimmer on the lids. This Deep Rose by G-Low is just right to add some fire to your eyes. Don't be shy with it, put on a good layer. Now at the inner and outer corners of the eye you want to blend in a slightly darker shade. The violet from the same Creative palette we used earlier is great. Now the liner. I know silver would be the obvious choice here, and I've seen that on, like, a load of tutorials, but we're going to have plenty of that elsewhere so I prefer a pale blue shimmer like this product by Maeve, in their summer line. Give it a good cat's eye, but don't worry if it's not exactly even here because this will all be blended so well.

Johnny had better pull in the advertising on this one. It's been five minutes and this is tired already. Who wants mermaid makeup when you can hang out with an actual fucking mermaid who can change their skin colour at will? Or be damn near fucking invisible?

Now, this is a new product you won't have seen before. I'll have the full details on my page but it's an exclusive! It's a super fine powder and it's mixed with these tiny holographic particles so you'll get an amazing shine. Get your kabuki brush and just go over really lightly on your upper cheekbones and around the jawline.

Then, we contour. You want a complimentary shade to your skin, but go a touch paler. You're going to paint it in here, and here, so about an inch below the eyes in a gentle curve, a touch on the forehead, a line down the nose and another dab on the chin, just under the lip. Now blend and blend and blend. I love these double-headed sponge blenders from Kuku Zhen which have little mermaid tails to hold them with! So cute.

Kill me now. Do you think the mermaids have the equivalent of a Peace Corps that you can join and get away from the world? Is that still a thing? My mother always went on about it. Yeah, me in scuba gear straddling a shark with a trident or whatever. Who knew the

Little Mermaid was so close and so fucking wrong? All Ursula and no Ariel.

Now the fun part. Get some fishnets, cut off the top of the stocking and just pull it over your head! Okay, so now we go for the more aqua shades, just go for harebell over turquoise to keep a bit of warm tone in it. So, I'm going back to the Creative palette again, and did you know if you purchase this palette you'll get half price on the foam-matte lip tint? That's such a bargain! So, with the kabuki brush again, just go round the hair line with the blue shades. Dab gently and blend as you go. Choose a few shades and just work it! Now I use this glitter powder blend by Mistique, and that highlights the cheekbones some more and picks out your other key features: chin, jawline, forehead. You're going angular here, don't be afraid of it. Be super careful when you take off the fishnet and you'll have perfect scales.

But don't look too closely. We all know they don't have scales on their faces and I keep having to do the fishnet crap because it's cheap and easy to pull off. Until you physically have to pull it off, when it will seventy percent of the time, guaranteed, ruin the last half hour.

I told you we would get to the silver. Now you can buy metallic contacts from most large makeup retailers these days but for this look I had an 'ocularist' make me up this amazing pair. I'm well practised putting these in, but if you're new to it you might want to get them in up front. You don't want to be crying all over that beautiful makeup you just put on! These are slightly pearlescent so they have that multicoloured sheen and a deep penetrating gaze of wisdom only a true mermaid believer can deliver!

That dead stare. That caught fish blank fucking look in their eyes, as if they've already been hit over the back of the head with a wooden priest. My uncle used to fish. The priest is like a tiny truncheon used for fish murder. He brought these trout over when he came to visit; gutted and frozen. He always left the heads on with those iced-over eyes staring at you as if they can see the fucking future or something. Always creeped me out. Now all I have paying the bills is these fucking mermaid makeovers and they're nothing like we were led to believe and those dead fish eyes feel like they're everywhere.

So, the lips. You're going to want to go plump and glossy. That foam-matte lip tint I was talking about earlier is just the thing. Give it a generous line. Plump it. This is the last step, so you can sip cocktails right up to this point! Now take a good look in the mirror, spritz with some holding spray. War. Huh!

And that's the creepiest thing about them. One kiss and their pheromones have you going cuckoo. As if I would ever want to be kissed by those over-plump fish lips. Johnny, you owe me big time for this.

The Sociologist

The oceans are vast. Man's experience starts with intertidal zones where the waters crash against cliffs; ooze over mudflats; crackle amongst pebbles; wash gently up and down white sands, accumulating a thick jetsam layer of driftwood, plastic, sea glass. At low tide we share the exposed flats with sea birds, pick our way over weed-slippery rocks and harvest stranded shells to serve them later with samphire and a bitter tomato jus. At high tide we throw in our lines, luring in the evening's predators and grilling them over open beach fires.

Some venture further for leisure. The icy morning swim to reinvigorate our flesh; snorkellers taking underwater selfies against a backdrop of shattered coral; divers mixing gases and risking nitrogen narcosis and embolisms and straight forward drowning in deeper and more claustrophobic wrecks, searching for ancient knowledge, salt-engraved tchotchkes and fame.

There are of course those who brave hurricanes and ocean swells to bring in larger game, and those whose preoccupation is simply to travel, to traverse the ocean as a singular feat of defiance against its force; or cruising in a gargantuan vessel loaded with the produce of modern commerce. But these types never intend to go below the waves.

That leaves the adventurers, fighters and explorers. The ones who drop into the inky depths to fix an oil leak; who lock themselves in submarines with encrypted orders and the stench of scared men; who beg for funding and sink in capsules bristling with sensors and cameras, hoping to catch a glimpse of something new and unique.

This last group have come the closest to discovering the secrets of the abyss. But for each new species of Atacama Snailfish, every octopus city and herbivorous shark, there are a billion more corners and nooks as yet untouched.

As a species we are loud, clumsy, polluting. It is easy for those below to see us coming, to take precautions, to hide themselves from our sight. This is how we missed the Clans.

The Hergowitz expedition was the first to publicly document what we now understand to be a vast population of Merfolk living in deep water areas worldwide. Of course, the ongoing war and the destruction of two of the expedition's vessels prevented much exploration into the Puerto Rico trench, but we saw for the first time what one might call the equivalent of outlying regions and villages. The social structure is essentially tribal, with decision making vested in elders. The Clans are proudly territorial. The now familiar footage from the expedition demonstrates the extent to which Merfolk have embraced farming and animal husbandry, sometimes on a grand scale. But the ocean floor and its resources are often the subject of dispute between Clans. As a result of the Merfolk's protandry, there is at least no gender-based inequality in their society, though there is apparently great reverence given to those who maintain an a-gendered state.

In addition to the Clans there are numerous nomadic tribes whose livelihood is dependent on trade between Clans. Some of the most extraordinary artwork discovered by the expedition was apparently the product of such trade, the artists unidentified. Little is known about these nomadic tribes, who are the most adept at blending into a myriad of underwater environments. The scientific theory is that they have more advanced chromatophores and are even better than the Merfolk of the Clans at simply disappearing. They have played little part in the fast evolving refugee crisis affecting the Atlantic Clans.

But how has the ongoing crisis affected our own society? As we adjust to the knowledge that Merfolk do exist and are now among us, how is society changing to accommodate this new species in our midst?

There is no question, as yet, of imposing a modern democratic society upon the Clans. Our main exposure has been to refugees from the ongoing war. We still have only a limited insight into the structure of Merfolk society and there is no indication how in any particular region democratic change might be effected, save through further warfare. Merfolk refugees have been reticent regarding their situation, and they are not yet here in sufficient numbers to promote an organised transition. Nevertheless, with every passing day more Merfolk come to our shores as word spreads that the land above is now taking in survivors.

What assistance would we be in such a transition? We have limited technology with which to even glimpse the depths in question, let alone conduct an effective counterstrike. This begs the further question regarding who to support in the war below. Governments have thus far refused to be drawn as to which side they believe to be in the right in the grand territorial dispute being conducted out in international waters. There has been more discussion of an international peace keeping force, but it is difficult to say how effective that might be when we have no real knowledge of the fighting methods and weaponry of the Merfolk. Some rumours have it that the cities have developed rudimentary projectile weapons. No concrete evidence has yet been seen of this, though some suggest the Hergowitz vessels were targeted in this way. More rife is speculation that there are platoons using sharks and whales even as tamed war beasts, and bound jellyfish as stinging weapons.

Inter-species communication raises unique possibilities, and we are gradually learning more from the Merfolk themselves. What is clear is that our society will forever be changed by knowledge of our cousins under the sea, and they will forever be changed by us. Whether that change is for better or worse remains to be seen.

The Producer

Pebbles crunched beneath my feet as we picked our way along Chesil Beach to the Sanctuary viewing station. I wished I'd worn sandals instead of my suede pumps, which would be all scuffed and salt-stained by the time we got there.

"Have you heard her sing yet?" I asked Dennis, my translator, who had obviously been here before and was mooching along in flip flops. He shook his head. "It's a treat," I said. "There are sounds she makes which can strip you to the bone and leave your soul exposed. You'll never hear anything like it. It's no wonder sailors used to dive in and drown at the sound."

"I'm looking forward to hearing it, I guess," he said, nonplussed. Meeting Celtique was just a paying gig to him. I could tell by his untucked shirt and overgrown toenails that the man had no passion. But after hearing her vocals recorded by a local diver, I was already obsessed with Celtique, and I knew the world would be too with the right promotion.

The viewing station was not much more than a shack, gaily painted to look like a beach hut. Despite fans whirring away the inside was warm and clammy. Most of one wall was taken up by the viewing screen. The offshore cameras were currently focused on a pair of cuttlefish wiggling stubby tentacles at each other as though they were having a dance off. There was a dull swishing sound as water churned past the underwater microphones. A Merfolk child swam by and waved.

"We're live," the technician said. "Wave back if you like, they love it."

I gave a cheery flick of my hand and the child darted away. I checked my watch. There was a digital clock set up by the underwater screen so Merfolk could keep appointments, but they weren't used to the concept of the twenty four hour clock and it was anyone's guess whether Celtique would actually show up.

I paced in the cramped space while Dennis sat playing with his phone. Then she appeared. Except she was a he, and he was bright blue and yellow. I only recognised him from the scarification on his shoulders which the diver had photographed. I'd been warned about the sex changing thing and the colour changing thing, but it was still a bit of a shock to me. Not to Dennis, who stood and smoothly signed a greeting. I cleared my throat and nodded to Dennis to begin translation.

"Hello Celtique. I'm Pamela Fabritz. Thank you for meeting me. I understand you like to sing?"

"Only when I'm female," Dennis translated.

"Ah. Yes. Would it be possible to, um, change for me?"

"Today I am hunting fish. Tomorrow I will be hunting fish. There is not enough food here. So I am male today. I will be male tomorrow."

"What if tomorrow, or soon, I could give you a new home with as much fish as you could ever want?"

"My family also need food. We need colder water. We need… He says, 'Being away with each other only'. Privacy. They need privacy."

"How many are in your family?"

"I have two partners and two children."

I had to stop and think for a moment. I hadn't expected such a large group, or that Merfolk were polyamorous. I would need a whole aquarium at this rate. But it could be worth it. An aquarium laced with web cams? Live coverage all day and all night. Their own network channel. Celtique and family. Move over Big Brother.

"We could make that work," I said, hoping the privacy thing wouldn't be too much of an issue for them once they were out of the Sanctuary. "I just need to hear you singing, then we can talk through all the details. Can you do that?"

He stared at the camera for a long moment then, just like a magic trick, shoulders narrowed and breasts and hips swelled and I was looking at the same Celtique I had a photograph of. Except for the colour.

I asked the technician to turn up the volume. The swell of the water intensified, and then there was another sound, a low keening, growing in strength. Notes in an exotic key undulated and swirled. The hairs on my arms stood up, and I found myself gaping.

"Dennis, what's she singing about? Ask her to sign." Dennis signed a few words, and we waited.

Celtique's voice filled the room with an alien opera. She began to sign as she sang, and Dennis whispered her words to me.

"Luminescence lights the blade.
I taste blood in the water.
Your colours dim.
I rush to you, but the current is strong.
You are swept up and away.
My heart sinks to the ocean floor.
I bury my heart in the sand,
And flee to the shallow waters
Where now you can never follow."

By the time Celtique's final notes had faded into the background sound of the sea, my face was wet with tears. After a brusque wipe with the back of my hand I started to applaud, and so did Dennis and the technician. I grinned. Celtique was perfect. Perhaps I could persuade her to sing something happier to start off with, but there was nothing like tapping into the soul of a war survivor to sway an audience. I could imagine whole arias of sorrow, layer upon layer of emotion, capturing the hearts of the whole world. Celtique singing in the Royal Albert Hall, and the next week singing for Oprah. There would be lucrative contracts pouring in, and all for the price of a few fish. What did Merfolk know about intellectual property?

But my thoughts had distracted me. I looked up at the screen again and saw that Celtique was not smiling. She signed for attention. Dennis gave me a hasty glance and then got back to work.

"I sing for you. I sing of my mother who was taken from us. Now it is only the five of us left. I want my family to survive. You can do this?"

"Absolutely," I replied.

The Child

Alua is my friend. They live in the house next door, which is not like our house but is all full of swimming pools. Mum says it's like the London Aquarium where we went one summer and saw all the fish and octopuses and penguins. Alua lives underwater, because they are Merfolk. Mum says I have to say 'they', because sometimes Alua is a girl like me and sometimes Alua is a boy. That's hard, because I don't like boys, but I do like Alua. I like it best when Alua is a girl. I think they know that because they are mostly a girl when I'm around. Alua has one brother-sister. Mum says the correct word is 'sibling'. They are older though and don't want to play with me.

I learned to swim at Alua's house. I can hold my breath now for nearly a whole minute. Not like Alua, who can hold their breath the whole time. They don't like it so much when they have to come up to the air, but they still keep me company when I'm swimming with them. I'm a good swimmer. I like back stroke best, but I can doggy paddle underwater now, even with my eyes open. You can't see much when you do that, though, it's all blurry. Alua swims mostly with their tail. They don't need to use their arms to move around. They can do the best things when they're swimming, like somersaults. I have a video of them I took on my phone. Do you want to see?

When I first met Alua we couldn't talk. We just waved at each other. Alua's parents are really rich, though, and they got a screen put underwater with videos on it so Alua could learn to sign. Mum says not a lot of Merfolk are rich but Alua's mum is a famous singer. Sometimes their mum is a man as well but Mum explained that because Celtique, that's Alua's mum, was a woman when they carried Alua in their tummy they will always be Alua's mum even when they are sometimes a man. So, Alua and I can talk to each other now. I had to have special lessons at school but there are more and more kids joining the class all the time. It's wow to be talking to Merfolk.

Some of the kids are not as nice about it. Jordan and Desi call them mean names like 'Fish' and 'No Legs'. Mum says they are 'perejudised', which is a long word to say they are boys being horrible boys. One time someone broke in to Alua's garden and put all sorts of nasty things in the water where the swimming pool goes from inside to outside. I remember when it happened because the next day there were police all over the place and there were lots of people in diving outfits going into the pool and bring out all manner of stuff: broken bottles and bricks and even a shopping trolley. I didn't see Alua that day, but I asked them about it later and they said they were very scared that someone would do that. I'm glad nobody has ever thrown anything in my swimming pool. I find a lot of dead bugs in there, though.

Alua can do more than swim. They can sing really well, just like their mum. They sing for me sometimes. I have to be underwater to hear them properly. It's hard to make out the words and I can't speak Merfolk anyway, but the tunes are always really pretty. Alua is always a girl when they sing. They say it's because when a Merfolk wants to make babies they become a woman and they sing their hearts out to make someone else want to become a man and make babies with them. I don't know why the women have to do the hard work but that's how it's done, and because of that I get to hear Alua singing. They tell me that soon they will be old enough to sing on TV. Celtique wants to keep them away from the TV for now, though, so they can grow up like a normal kid.

I have asked Alua about their world in the sea where they came from. They don't like to talk about it. I think they have bad dreams sometimes about what happened there. Sometimes I have bad dreams just thinking about it, because they lived with sharks and whales and all sorts of dangerous stinging jellyfish. Alua says that it wasn't all bad, though. They had a fish as a pet once which had a light hanging in front of its face and could show them the way in the dark.

They had lots of friends and there was no school for them to go to, they just played in the sea and watched their parents and copied what they did to learn stuff. They could change colour to hide from each other, like playing hide and seek. Did I say that Alua can change colour? They are mostly a nice purple colour, though.

I'm hoping that soon Alua will be able to come to school with me. Mum says they are making things called 'pods' which are like plastic water tanks on wheels so that Merfolk can move around more easily. The pods are see-through so the Merfolk can see what's happening around them, and we can see them signing. There are controls in the pod that a Merfolk can move with their tails, sort of like a joystick that makes the pod move, and they have something like gloves so that Merfolk can put their hands out and touch things. I want Alua to come with me to Show and Tell. They can look at Jordan and Desi right in the eye and flick salty water at them. Or maybe one day Alua can come and be next to me in class and help me with my maths homework. One thing I know is that she will always be my friend. Can you say you have a Merfolk as a friend?

The Journalist

He Left Me For a Mermaid!
Devastated soap star tells all in shocking exclusive!

Tanya Crezowski, beloved star of TV's 'Stormy Weather', was left heartbroken last week as long-term partner, Brin Daniels, abandoned her. Crezowski, 31, had been with Daniels, 35, for seven years and thought the time was coming when he might propose. Instead, to her horror, Daniels told her last week he was leaving her for a mermaid.

Crezowski wept as she spoke exclusively to our reporter about her nightmare. The couple met when Crezowski was 24, before she got her first big break. After early success in her role as sultry femme fatale Jessica Tindall, Crezowski bought a countryside home in Surrey and soon invited Daniels to move in with her. "We were so good together," she said. "I had this life planned in my head. We were going to marry, have children, and grow old together. Now that's all ruined."

The BAFTA nominated actress could have had her pick of the rich and famous, but instead chose to stay with Daniels as her own fame grew. Daniels, an architect, might have seemed an odd choice for such a celebrated star. But how he came to leave her was even stranger.

"When I first heard about Merfolk I was as excited as everyone," Crezowski told us. "Who wouldn't be? They were like straight out of a fantasy world. I don't know what I expected, perhaps Disney princesses, but they're nothing like that in real life. Merfolk are half animal, and it shows." We all know now that Merfolk are war-mongering creatures, but little did Crezowski know that she would end up in battle with one.

Daniels was invited to design a bespoke home for a group of Merfolk leaving the Sanctuary refugee centre off the coast of Dorset. He spent a considerable amount of time at the site while it was built, and kept coming back afterwards, telling Crezowski he had to oversee all the finishing touches as the Merfolk moved in. "I should have realised something was wrong when he was away from home so much, and the fact he never talked about the Merfolk that he met should have been a red flag. But I never suspected he would cheat on me, least of all that he would leave me for a Fish!"

It turns out Daniels was learning to sign and was getting to know one of his clients a little too well. A neighbour told us, "I saw him regularly swimming with the Merfolk in their outdoor pool. It's hard to tell them apart but there was one he seemed attached to; a female who liked to turn dark green. She wouldn't spend long with her head above water but when she did, he was there stroking her hair and touching her arms. He wouldn't leave her alone."

Crezowski is convinced her lover has been duped by the mermaid. "Touching them does things to you," she said. "How do I know he isn't under some spell?" How indeed? Our advice is to lock up your lovers, husbands and sons around these creatures. The slightest touch from a mermaid and you might never see them again.

Celtique In Mad Splash For Sponsor's Cash
Greedy Merfolk set to sue over web-cam row

Rescued Merfolk Celtique was in the public eye earlier this year when their debut single topped both the popular and classical charts. They owe it all to producer and entrepreneur Pamela Fabritz who freed Celtique from the drudgery of the Sanctuary and brought them into the limelight. TV viewers have enjoyed seeing Celtique and their family of Merfolk as they go about their luxury underwater lives. Fabritz spared no cost in ensuring that the family had everything they could ever want in their new home. Now they have come to blows over the terms of their business arrangement.

Celtique's legal team claim that the family was not told they would be stars of their own TV show. The ludicrous suggestion came at a time when Celtique, their two partners and two children had already been on air for over three months. The lawyers claim that Celtique was unaware that there were web-cams in the house until Celtique had a magazine interview where they were asked about the show.

Fabritz is saddened by the news that Celtique will now be seeking an injunction to stop filming, and damages for alleged unpaid wages for the family's participation to date.

"When I first met Celtique they would have done anything to get their family away from their poor life as refugees. I took pity on them. I provided them with a home and a life they could never have dreamed of, a million miles away from the war-torn ocean they left behind. They had the finest food and the best education for their children. Celtique wore pearls I paid for and had access to a huge audience thanks to me. That's what propelled her to her number one hit. That was my hard work. We didn't have any binding contract – how can you make a contract with an animal? – but I did it all out of trust and gave them everything they asked for and needed. Now that's all been thrown back in my face."

Fabritz's view of the Merfolk is shared by many. There has been anger online, with one Twitter user commenting, "Get back to the ocean Celtique. So long, Fish, and thanks for nothing." This echoes calls made for the Government to tighten Merfolk immigration laws and the rules under which Merfolk can be sponsored to come onto the mainland. An anonymous source in Whitehall said, "Sponsors take on a huge risk and great expense when they allow a Merfolk into their lives. We are looking at ways to prevent exploitation of sponsors by the Merfolk they save. The Merfolk Recognition Act already allows for deportation measures where Merfolk are guilty of crimes, but we need to consider extending those laws to protect sponsors."

The injunction hearing will take place in the High Court next week. We will bring you all the latest!

The Artist

I squeeze clay between my fingers. Through pod's skin it is slippery, like eel. I prefer to work in water, but this man substance drifts away in red-brown clouds. So I use the pod, sealing my body in its walls, putting my hands into plastic the shape of hands so I can work in air. Plastic is new to me. It is more man substance, clear like water, tough like skin of teeth-beast, sometimes hard and sometimes thin and soft. I would like to make it into new shapes, but I do not yet know how.

Clay I can shape. I make the shape of bone of great one. It is smooth and as long as my arm. With a small stick I carve symbols for death. Death of great one I will never see again. Death of my home beneath the waves. I smooth an error with my finger, carve again. The clay is not like stones from the ocean. It can change and change again. I make and remake the bone as I make and remake myself.

Today, male, I. My colour is red, and I make gold circles down my arms. My new family, the Morgensterns, say I am art, sometimes more than pieces I make for them. They make art of me. With a machine they take my image. They display it back to me on screens. I see my face and on the screen I look sad.

I should not feel sad. I have a new life now, where I can at least create. I am not attacked. I am not hunting. I just create my art. But there is emptiness in my new life. I miss the ocean. I miss great swell of currents, heat of vents on ocean floor, sound of great ones passing by. I miss other Merfolk, even sometimes those trying to kill me. There is no urgency here. Less alive, I. Lonely.

The Morgensterns are some company, but they are strange. My pool is small, but they swim in it. They do not ask. Like a pet to them, I. They see me as a thing which belongs to them. Sometimes they want me to come into my pod and be with them in the air. Many people gather. They eat and drink and after a few waves they become loud and stumble. They sign badly, or just watch me without trying to talk at all. Art, I, to be watched and not to speak back.

Sometimes other artists come to talk with me. They want to understand Merfolk symbols. They sign fast and point at my art and ask me to explain. I carve for them. I show symbols for peace, and for war. I show health, then death. I show love. Mother. Change. In return I learn writing, which is man's way of marking symbols but for many words. They teach me how to carve my name, Tomasin. Writing is ugly. My name looks ugly. I do not carve it again.

They show me pictures they make, and on their screens art from many people. Man's art is strange. It is mostly flat. I see shapes I do not understand, patterns I would love to put on my skin, images of things that cannot be. I have learned a new language. Cubism. To take an image on a rock and shatter it into many pieces and rearrange it again, sometimes facing the right way and sometimes the wrong way. I see my heart, broken in so many pieces and rearranged by this odd new world. Perspective. The art of making things look as though they are seen from far away, while other things appear so close you could touch them. I feel the agony of things I can no longer touch.

They teach me new words, new grammar, new ways of thinking. I learn the word for 'inspire'. An inspiration to these artists, I. They have never seen my kind of work before. Shapes of tides and shadows of a coral fan and symbols of belonging or happiness seem so natural to me, but the whorls and swirls of my work are new to them and a kind of wonder. In turn their art inspires me. I make circles like Kandinsky on my chest and artists are wild. They bring Eva Morgenstern and her hands fly to her face with such joy. She brings out her machine and takes my image again. Others hold up their machines and later they will show me moving pictures of myself.

In these moments I feel less alone. But still watched, I. I will never be one of them. We have the same heart. We have different skin.

Ida Keogh

Today I am female. I have huge rock from the ocean floor. A surprise. A treat. I can work on it in my pool with so many tools Eva has brought for me. She tells me this piece is important. I feel its shape. It has sharp scent. I see in it the curves of a great squid, fighting with a Merfolk. It is symbol of war. The war I have escaped, but which still attacks my mind. I strike and feel rock break. I strike again and again. Each blow is a release. I did not know I had become so angry. In my design the Merfolk is squeezed by tentacles. They cannot move except to thrash their tail. Their head is flung back and their mouth is open wide in a death song. I realise this is how I feel. The war has trapped me here. I have a better life than I had in the Sanctuary where all Merfolk were piled together, but I miss the ocean.

I become deepest blue, the colour of the ocean at night. I score lines and circles, curves and scales, until my work is finished. Tomorrow I will carve something new.

The Politician

Merfolk Resettlement
Debated on 2 April 2026

Charles Fitzsimmons >
(South Dorset)(Con)

South Dorset is host to the Sanctuary, the largest and most densely populated refugee camp for Merfolk in the United Kingdom. In 2025 only three percent of the Merfolk population at the Sanctuary were resettled in sponsored accommodation on the mainland, five percent were resettled in other European countries and none were relocated back to the Atlantic Ocean. There has been a significant environmental impact on the Chesil Beach area in terms of pollution of our waters and decimation of our fish stocks. There has further been a knock-on effect on tourism to both Chesil Beach and Portland, which has been negatively impacted by proximity to the site. These hidden costs of accommodating the camp are not covered by the governmental fund provided to South Dorset for the running of the site and must be borne by increases in local Council Tax. As the minister tasked with coordinating the government response to the Merfolk crisis and arranging the permanent resettlement of the occupants of the Sanctuary, what support will my Honourable Friend be offering to South Dorset to ameliorate the financial pressures caused by Merfolk immigration in this area?

The Parliamentary Under-Secretary of State for the Home Department > (Claire Underbrook)

My Honourable Friend rightly points out the significant impact which Merfolk have on our economy both directly and indirectly. The United Kingdom is a world leader in resettlement and has successfully rehomed over one thousand two hundred Merfolk from refugee camps in the last three years. Over half of those have been removed to other locations in Europe. My Right Honourable Friend the Home Secretary continues to negotiate with our European counterparts in relation to this issue and it is hoped that a revised Treaty will soon be forthcoming.

Simon Aulden >
(Great Grimsby)(Con)

In relation to the continuing negotiations with Europe, we have seen so many times that Europe gives with one hand

and takes with the other. My Honourable Friend rightly champions the efforts made to resettle Merfolk in the waters of other European countries, but what assurances can she give that her department will address in the revised Treaty the need to revisit fishing quotas which have not been amended since the Merfolk crisis commenced? Our fish stocks are rapidly diminishing as a result of Merfolk gorging on our local supplies, and those stocks which would have fed the British public are being redeployed to feed the growing numbers of Merfolk held in refugee camps. I understand that many parts of the United Kingdom are importing over fifty percent of fish from international suppliers at a time when the average price of seafood is increasing exponentially. How will my Right Honourable Friend the Home Secretary regain control of our fish?

Claire Underbrook >

The impact of the Merfolk population on fish stocks has been dramatic and is of course something my Right Honourable Friend the Home Secretary will wish to address in her negotiations. The question of fish quotas is not part of my portfolio, but I recognise the urgent need to take back control of our waters. To that end I am proud to announce that this department is also planning to commence negotiations with Europe, the United States and other key international players to found a refuge in the Atlantic Ocean where Merfolk from across Europe can be permanently resettled. This will not be an easy task given the continuing warfare in the area, but the ultimate goal of repatriating Merfolk to their natural habitat is one which we will make every effort to strive towards.

Bethany Smith >
(Brentford and Isleworth)(Lab)

London has the densest population of land-settled Merfolk in the UK, and my constituents have welcomed our underwater cousins with open arms. They are singers, artists, chefs, consultants, translators. But more than that they are colleagues, neighbours and friends. They have created a new market in property redevelopment and have stimulated growth in several key economic areas. Yet these important members of our community are vilified and treated with contempt by the present government. The Merfolk Recognition Act 2023 continues to be used punitively and Merfolk are detained and deported for the most minor infractions. They are taken back to places like the Sanctuary, where Merfolk experience extreme poverty and restriction of their freedom. The government has most recently announced plans for stricter controls on the regulation of sponsored Merfolk, which accounts for the vast majority of those resettled on the mainland. When will my Honourable Friend's department start to recognise the positive benefit

Merfolk have in our communities? She surely cannot avoid the fact that Merfolk have escaped warfare and risk everything to come to the shallow waters of the UK, only to be treated as less than second class citizens and more like animals. When will this government commit to improved rights for Merfolk, both those who remain destitute in our refugee camps and those who are fortunate enough to treat our communities as a new home?

Claire Underbrook >

The Member of Parliament for Brentford and Isleworth forgets that as an island nation Great Britain has seen the greatest influx of Merfolk in Europe. Our borders are overrun, and it is at prohibitive cost that we fund coastal refugee camps to provide protection and a basic level of subsistence for thousands of Merfolk. Despite our misgivings about this relatively unknown but undoubtedly hostile and war-like race, this government commenced a sponsorship programme to lift the most gifted Merfolk to join us in our communities and to work alongside us. But when they take that for granted, when they flout our laws and exploit their sponsors, this government will stand strong and ensure that those Merfolk who cannot live with us are returned to the sea. We will not abandon those who have given so generously in permitting Merfolk into their homes and into their businesses. Our first priority must always be to our human citizens!

The Therapist

I keep seeing the knife going into their chest. Blood clouds in the water. For a moment, the colour matches their skin, then they start to fade to pale brown as the blood keeps spreading. There is so much blood. I can taste it.

Stephan took a note, cramped letters marking a blue page. Meets diagnostic criteria for post-traumatic stress disorder. Vivid flashbacks. Obsession with blood. He clicked his pen three times, then set it down.

He had dealt with veterans in the past, listened to harrowing stories of bombings, guilt at targeting the innocent, the shock of comrades falling in gunfire. But he had rarely dealt with stabbings, because soldiers rarely had such close contact with the enemy. Modern warfare increasingly preferred drone strikes to feet on the ground. It was also preferable from a psychological perspective. The further a soldier's remove from the actual victim of their attack the easier it was to launch it. Pressing a button was easier than firing a gun. Pulling a trigger was easier than stabbing. The act of plunging a knife through skin and muscle was visceral, almost sexual in its intimacy.

The Merfolk, Verien, swam to the back of the tank. Her deep green skin flashed momentarily with blue. A passing thought, or another memory perhaps. Stephan waited for her to return. Her, not they, because she only presented as female now. She had not been male since the battle and could not bear the thought of transforming again. Something else she and Stephan would need to work on together, in time.

"What happened to the body, Verien?" he said, signing at the same time. It didn't help the Merfolk for him to speak but it was better than having a whole session in silence.

Verien's face flashed with anger, and she struck the glass of the tank with a curled fist.

They were the enemy! I watched their body fall to the ocean floor. It raised plumes of grey sand. Their eyes stayed open, staring up at me. I saw a teeth-beast coming and I turned away.

"How many more did you kill that day?"

None. I have killed no more since. I felt sick. I could not go back to the fight. I swam away and hid in the caves, but the enemy threw great rocks and destroyed much of the city. That night I abandoned my armour and became female. I joined those fleeing to the shallows. We spent days hiding in fields of weed with nothing to eat, terrified the enemy would chase us. I became dark green to match the plants which saved us.

"Is that why you prefer to stay that colour? Does it feel safer?"

Verien made a vague gesture with her hand. Stephan scribbled another note. There was the end of the scene. But how to take the pain from it? At this point Stephan would normally pull out all his best relaxation techniques, then invite a client to imagine they were in a cinema, watching events unfold on the big screen. With closed eyes, he would ask them to watch the film forwards, then imagine it running backwards. Forwards again, but in black and white. Backwards, in black and white. Forwards, in black and white but now on a small television screen. Backwards again. The picture vanishing slowly, to a white dot, then disappearing. But Merfolk were not renowned for their cinema going habits. Would Verien even understand the concept of black and white? No, a different approach would be needed.

"Tell me about your partner. Have you spoken to him about the war?"

Brin is understanding. He is a good man. Do you know he designed this house? That's how we met. I tell him what he needs to hear, that although I have killed I am not dangerous to him. I would not hurt him.

"Do you ever feel like hurting yourself?"

Verien looked up suddenly and her hair floated around her face like a veil. *It is tradition, after war, to carve symbols of peace. To show you have survived. To show you will not harm again. But I cannot. Even this act of carving into my own skin is too much*

66

blood for me to bear. I think of hurting myself every day, but I cannot use a knife. I do not even use one to eat with. Brin has fish delivered to me already cut. I feel like a child, not able to cut my own food. But better that than to hold a knife in my hands again.

The pen clicked. Suicidal ideation. Avoidance. "Do you have other friends who can support you?"

I live in a collective with six other Merfolk. They have their own issues to deal with, but they help me as best they can. Three are joined, so they are close and have little time for the rest of us. My closest friend, Genono, leaves to start their own business enticing humans. The other two are good friends to me, but they left the city before the trouble started and do not understand what it is like to have been in war. I have no human friends except Brin. His friends have abandoned him since he joined with me. He cannot understand, either, what it is to take a life.

"Was it difficult? Taking a life?"

That is the problem I have every tide. It is the most difficult thing I have ever done. But in the moment I did it, it was easy. I was defending myself. It came naturally to me. I hate myself for that.

Stephan made another note. They bleed. They fight. Their survival instinct is a natural driving force. They must escape from each other, and when they survive, they are afraid. They hold those fears close to them, years after the cause of the trauma has passed. When it comes down to it, they think the same way we do.

The Taxi Driver

"Where to, mate?"

"Kingsway, please."

"Sure. Sorry about the squeeze in the back there, mate, the whole lot had to be pushed forward to make way for pods, ya know. Can't run a black cab nowadays without space for Merfolk. Sad times. My old man ran a cab donkey's years, not a Merfolk in sight back then. Nice to see a pair of legs in my cab."

"This used to be a six-seater?"

"Yeah, it was a classic. Only a few of them about now, what with the unions insisting we all take on Fish passengers."

"You know, it's probably best not to use the term 'Fish' when you're taking customers."

"Really, mate? I take them when they need it. Got a new hoist fitted, they can go wherever. If they don't pay, I can drop 'em in the Thames! Only kidding. I hear they're not all that fond of fresh water. Brings them out in a rash, I guess. So, what's your business today? Above or below the waves?"

"Below. Not literally, but I'm meeting a Merfolk client."

"Ah. Yeah, I see, mate. It's everywhere now, innit. This time five years ago you'd be on your way to a board meeting for, what? Finance? Telecommunications? Now it's all about the pearl trade, underwater timeshares and fahking sushi restaurants with a salt pool. Can't make a decent coin nowadays without treading on someone's tail."

"Actually, I'm a barrister. I'm concerned with Merfolk rights."

"Lawyer, huh? Must be interesting. Don't get me wrong, I'm sure they're entitled to rights and what not, but what with all this new guidance we have to follow it's costing me a fortune. I reckon the whole economy is going down the swanny with it all."

"Some would say we've been enriched by our new friends. There are whole new trade sectors opening up, and surely it's more business for you too?"

"You think? Nah, mate. Our economy was perfectly fine before they came along. Golden. You think it's better? Try being a cabbie. Cost an arm and a leg converting this baby, and for what? So I can lug rich Fish about between London clubs with brand new basement swimming pools? You don't know the half of it, mate."

"It's not only about the Merfolk with money. Ordinary Merfolk need transport just as much. More so perhaps, as they don't have the luxury of private vehicles and chauffeurs. Do you want to know what it's like living on oceanic refugee benefits?"

"Nah, I'm not sure I do want to know. No disrespect, mate, but whatever you're doing for them I'm not interested. I just hope you're getting paid proper. They don't even know what a pound is. Had one of them in my cab tried to pay me with fahking seashells. Told me they was rare. Like, what am I going to do with that crap? If it's not got contactless, I'm not interested mate. And if they're on benefits that's my tax money paying for it."

"You should have taken the shells. The trade-in market is good, they're considered cultural artefacts. Rarities are worth more than a dozen cab rides. If you're ever offered pearls by the way you should definitely take them – it's hugely disrespectful to decline."

"Look, their culture is not the issue here. They live here now; they need to get along. I've had to learn all the sign language and stuff; they need to have a bit of respect for the way we do things around here. I don't want ritual symbols carved in my leather for luck, right? I don't give a shit about pearls and I cannot fahking stand those grim statues. Give me the right creeps, they do."

"You mean basalt carvings? I've seen some really beautiful examples at the Tate Modern. Perhaps you should try the exhibition some time. Personally, I believe their art is superb."

"Seriously, you like all that shit? Well, that's up to you, mate. I bet you've got lots of that 'art' in your house, have you?"

"I have a couple of small pieces, and I've started a shell collection. Gifts, mostly."

"Ahh, I thought so! Do you still have pictures of your kids up or is everything covered in salt now?"

"I don't have children. But in any event, I don't see why their art can't stand alongside traditional human pieces. The creativity of the Merfolk is to be celebrated and embraced, in my view."

"Yeah, I'm not saying it's all bad. There's that Celtique, the singing one, she's interesting. I like that thing she did with the whale song."

"Is that the one where it sounds like they're doing a duet with a blue whale? It's uncanny, isn't it."

"Yeah, that's the one. You're one of those that calls the Fish 'they', are you? I can't get used to it, mate. If it looks like a bird, it's a she. If it looks like a bloke, it's a bloke. All that gender swapping, it's not natural."

"It's perfectly natural for them. Protandry is not an uncommon trait in underwater species."

"What's that? Well, I'm not sure I care if it's natural for them, it's just weird, innit? Bird one day, bloke the next. Don't know who you're dealing with, do you?"

"They're still the same person, whatever gender they choose. Celtique prefers to be known by a neutral gender term. There are also those who choose to be neither male nor female all the time, resting in between genders. Have you met an a-gendered Merfolk?"

"Not yet, though I imagine it will happen sooner or later, I've seen enough weird stuff already that nothing would surprise me now."

"I hope you'll show a little understanding when you do. They are revered in Merfolk culture."

"All right mate, you've given me something to think about. I promise if I meet an in between Fish I'll treat them extra nice."

"This is me, here. Keep the change."

"Cheers, mate, have a good day."

"Where to, love? Sorry about the squeeze in the back there..."

The Barrister

Counsel For The Claimant, Mr Greene: Madam, the preliminary issue before you is one of considerable importance. This is the first claim brought by a Merfolk under the auspices of the Equality Act 2010 in relation to discrimination at work. It is acknowledged that the potential consequences of allowing the claim to proceed, or indeed of halting it at this stage, are far reaching. The claim is likely to be relied upon as a test case for the many hundreds of Merfolk now in private employment in the United Kingdom and for their employers.

That is not to say that discrimination against Merfolk is necessarily widespread across all employment sectors. The offer of private work to Merfolk is to be lauded generally as a positive step towards their integration into our society. But it must be recognised that discrimination does exist, and where such a grotesque situation arises it has the potential to cause considerable upset and harm. The question before you today is whether such harm is to be protected against in law, or whether it should be permitted to continue unchecked.

The facts of the present case remain firmly in dispute and will be a matter for a full trial if the claim is allowed to proceed. However, for present purposes it should be assumed that the facts stated in the claim form are true.

Shariste is a Merfolk who fled from the Atlantic wars in 2025, some years after Merfolk were first discovered and at a time when various institutions had been put in place to manage the increasing Merfolk population around the shores of the UK. Shariste stayed for a time at the renowned refugee camp off the coast of Dorset, the Sanctuary. They learned to sign and were keen to join those Merfolk who had already moved onto land.

Shariste has always had a love for food. They are an aficionado of traditional Merfolk cuisine. It is no surprise that they were recruited to become a chef. They were sponsored by the newly formed Ningyo chain of restaurants along with a number of other Merfolk. After a period of training with their peers, Shariste was selected to become sous chef at Ningyo's flagship restaurant in central London. This is a position which ought to have brought considerable pride and satisfaction, but instead brought a period of intense suffering and hardship at the hands of their colleagues, and in particular the head chef Mr Campina and manager Mr Smyth.

From the outset of their employment relationship, Mr Smyth insisted that Shariste should present as female and only female. He told Shariste that staff found it confusing for them to be switching genders and requiring the use of 'they' pronouns. As a result, the staff all referred to Shariste as she/her.

In their female state, Shariste caught the unwanted attention of Mr Campina. He regularly made lewd comments and gestures towards them, as set out in full in the Particulars of Claim. In the most serious incident on 15 January 2027, when Shariste was working in a pod at the restaurant, he grabbed their gloved hand and placed it on his crotch. When they pulled away he called them a 'Filthy Fish'. From that day on Shariste was ostracised by Mr Campina. When they complained to Mr Smyth about Mr Campina's conduct, Mr Smyth's response was to hold a disciplinary hearing at which Shariste was accused of insubordination. Her contract was terminated.

Shariste brought these proceedings with the assistance of a charitable organisation. You are aware, Madam, that I appear before you today on a pro bono basis. The claim is for harassment on grounds of race and sexual harassment. The response to the claim contends that the Tribunal has no jurisdiction to entertain a claim brought by a Merfolk. It is baldly asserted that the protections offered by the Equality Act 2010 are for humans only.

Under section 9 of the Equality Act 2010, race includes colour, nationality and ethnic or national origins. Under section 26, a person (A) harasses another (B) if A engages in unwanted conduct related to a relevant protected characteristic, which includes race, and the conduct has the purpose or effect of violating B's dignity, or creating an intimidating, hostile, degrading, humiliating or offensive environment for B. A also harasses B if A engages in unwanted conduct of a sexual nature which has the same purpose or effect.

The two issues for you today are whether Shariste is a 'person' within the meaning of section 26, and whether being Merfolk is sufficient to constitute a racial group. Shariste contends that the answer to the second question is obvious. As a separate species, Merfolk must be a distinct racial group.

As to the first question, Madam, the starting point is the Merfolk Recognition Act 2023. The Act was introduced ostensibly to create criminal liability for Merfolk. It recognises Merfolk as 'persons' for the purpose of criminal law.

The question whether the ambit of the Act can be extended for other legal purposes was considered in the case of *Celtique v Fabritz Productions Ltd* [2024] 1 WLR 367. That case involved the Merfolk singer, Celtique, who successfully brought proceedings against Fabritz Productions for breach of contract. Lord Ododjo in the Court of Appeal stated in that case, "The law is a patchwork quilt, with criminal liabilities and civil liberties stitched side by side. Parliament cannot have intended for us to attempt to unpick those stitches and class Merfolk as persons for some patches but not all. If they are subject to punitive measures should they commit a crime, then surely they should also be afforded protections when crimes are committed against them. It is only a short step from there to say that they should enjoy the full benefits of our legal system."

Madam, this judgment is binding upon the Tribunal, and is clear authority that Merfolk should be considered legal persons for the purposes of the Equality Act 2010. I ask that justice is done today, for the benefit of all, and not to the exclusion of Merfolk who are a valuable asset to our society.

Unless I can assist you further, those are my submissions.

The Sex Worker

The man floats in water in front of me. Naked, except for his mask and air machine. Tube coils into his mouth like eel. Bubbles rise. He breathes heavily. I dance for him. My body describes a spiral, my tail flicking so he will feel small waves hitting his chest. I move my arms slowly, running my hands down my sides and up through my hair. I become a rainbow of colour, pale pinks, blues and yellows. My clients like that combination best.

He moves towards me, hands stretched out. I circle around him, teasing. He has paid a lot of money to be here in my tank, to watch me dance, to touch me. I make him wait a little longer. I swim beneath him, then come up between his arms. He grabs hold of me immediately, his hands gripping my waist. I twist and swim out of his reach. I wait for him to calm again, then move just close enough for him to touch scars on my chest. His fingers trace their lines. They feel rough against my skin. I raise my arms and his hands trail down their length.

As soon as he touches my wrists he goes into a frenzy. Like teeth-beast when there is blood in the water. He launches himself towards me and rips the tube from his mouth. They always do this. As if they forget they have to breathe. I coil myself around him and put my mouth to his, give him air. I feel him stiffen against me. I move my hand down. One touch is all it takes. He groans into my mouth and his body shudders, then goes limp. Done, my work. I lift him to the surface. He gasps in the air. I watch him float for a while to make sure he breathes and will not try to swim down to me again, then I leave him to climb out of the tank himself. I watch him dress through the glass. He presses a hand against the tank in farewell.

I will do this two more times this morning, then this afternoon I will be on the screen. My sponsor, Samantha, put a camera in my tank, which is a machine for making images. Many people watch me dance, and they all pay. Samantha says I will have to do this for another two years, then my home will be paid for. Many tides, a year. But this work I can do.

I learned when I arrived in the shallows. Captured, I. Made to work in small tank and in dirty water. They used something to give me a shock if I tried to become male. Samantha told me about electricity, which is a dangerous and powerful thing humans use to make machines work. The people who captured me forced me to dance with men. It was not many tides, but frightened, I. Police rescued me.

They are humans who take control over others. I could not sign then, and neither could police. From one tank to another they moved me, and eventually took me to the Sanctuary. That is where Samantha found me. She asked if I could do it again, enticing men. But this time on my own terms, and for money. I decided I will make money from humans and I will become independent.

My name is Genono, but Samantha tells me on the screen they call me Marina. She does not use my real name. Samantha used to do what I do. She used to entice men. She was called Scarlet, which is a type of red. She invites women to the house to speak with me. They tell me of their stories, of violent men and unsafe streets. I am lucky I have my own home to work from. Men have not attacked me, not since I was first captured, and I can become male if they do. These women must take risks if they want work. I suggest to Samantha that they could sometimes work from my home, to keep them safe. But this is not allowed. My home would become a brothel, which is a place forbidden by police. Samantha says the work I do must be kept secret. It is allowed for me to do it, but it is not allowed for her to help me. But she can help people watch me dance. They must watch me on the screen many times before they are invited to meet me. She helps other women in the same way. Safer for them, she says, even though she puts herself at risk of being taken by the police. I do not understand the rules. But I am safe at least, and one day I will be free.

Samantha has taught me how to use a screen underwater. I touch it and it makes pictures and words. I am learning to read human language. It is hard, and there are many things I do not understand. Most Merfolk have learned to sign but I think very few are taught to write. Samantha is different. She says she will help me, then one day I can help others. I would like to teach other Merfolk to read and write. When I have enough money that I don't have to dance any more I will create a school for Merfolk. When we have the skill of human language we can do anything. I could teach children, and when they grow up they could heal the sick with human knowledge, teach humans how to speak with teeth-beasts and great ones, build cities of water on the land.

Just two more years, then I will not owe money to anyone. My home will be my own. I will have the money to start teaching. Until then, I will learn, and I will dance.

The Missionary

I sat on the edge of the rib, one hand clasped against my regulator, the other clutching my Bible in its waterproof pouch. I had trained for this moment. Not just the scuba diving, though days in a cold swimming pool and then exploring Stoney Cove reservoir had been gruelling enough. Not just learning Merfolk sign language, which I still struggled with. I had trained to become the United Kingdom's first Merfolk missionary. The newly founded Church of the Subaquatic would make the first forays underwater to visit Merfolk in their own territory. We were awaiting funding to stage a deep sea expedition, but in the meantime there was a captive audience of Merfolk just off the English coast. What they needed was an ordained vicar, and I was selected out of dozens of applicants. So it was with a little pride, of which I should have been ashamed, that I waited to plunge into the waters of the Sanctuary.

I was nervous. The water was choppy and grey despite the sunny day. But I remembered my Psalms, 'Mightier than the waves of the sea is His love for you.' I could do this. I took a deep breath and tipped backwards. The cold hit my face with a rush of bubbles. Water seeped under my hood as I bobbed back up to the surface. I gave the okay sign to my assigned buddy, Geoff, then pushed the button on my chest to purge air from my dry suit and descend. I felt pressure building in my ears, so I squeezed my nose and blew gently to equalise. I watched my depth gauge. Six metres. Nine. Twelve. The sea floor was around twenty metres. I slowed my descent as magenta anemone-covered boulders came into view. I accidentally kicked up a plume of sand and waved it from my face as I sunk to my knees. Geoff arrived a moment later, floating perfectly. He swam over to a nearby pile of rocks and shone his torch on the largest crab I have ever seen. He pointed to it, making little pincer movements with his hands. If it weren't for his regulator I would say he was laughing. But there was only one kind of wildlife I was here to see. I signed to Geoff. *Where are they all?* Geoff motioned for me to follow him. I swam after him, accompanied by little puffs and hisses of air as I tried to get my buoyancy right.

I knew we had found the church the second I saw it. A formation of granite rocks formed a small cove. Light was shining down in shafts which made the sand appear to move and glitter. But best of all, it was full of Merfolk.

This was my moment. I swam through the waiting congregation as though down a church aisle, pleased as punch. I had no idea of course whether the Merfolk were here to see me or simply here because it was a natural gathering spot. I would soon find out. I turned to face them all, then began to sign.

Greetings my friends and welcome! I bring tidings of great joy. The Lord is come to you!

I wish I could say that in that moment a hush fell upon the water and the faces of the Merfolk present lit up with His holy light. But they all ignored me. I looked at my air gauge. Was my tank half full, or half empty? I took a deep breath and felt myself rise a little in the water. I had not come here to give up so easily. One or two Merfolk were eyeing me curiously. That was a good enough starting point. I went through the mental list I had prepared of the relevant Psalms. I was a little concerned about appealing to their vanity but Psalms 139:14 seemed a good way to engage them. I waved my arms in the water to attract the attention of a few more Merfolk, then began to sign again. *You are beautiful, for you are fearfully and wonderfully made! Yes, I am talking to you, and about you. The Lord made you just as he made me, just as he made this sea and all the creatures in it.*

One of the Merfolk cocked their head, a gesture so human it took me aback for a moment. I had to remind myself of Genesis 1:26: these creatures, wondrous though they were, had not been created in the image of God as humans were. They were a simulacrum from the waist up, and fish from the waist down. But they were intelligent, and could therefore be worthy of God's love if they learned to give up their warlike ways. I could not work out whether the Merfolk was male or female by looking at it. I had been warned that some stayed in-between genders, and this seemed to be such a one. I gestured for it to come to me, and it did.

I have a message for you! The Bible tells us that as in water face reflects face, so the heart of man reflects the man. Are you pure in heart?

The Merfolk looked at me and looked lost in thought for a moment. Then it signed back to me. *Only the surface of water reflects. Men say that they are good, but we see this often only on the surface. How can I know what lies in your heart?*

This confounded me. I replied as best I could. *I am a vicar. My sins have been forgiven by the Lord and my heart is pure. I come to teach you the word of the Lord so your sins may also be forgiven.*

You have not seen war. What do you know of sin? Now others had gathered and were watching our discourse. This was my chance.

I can teach you of sin and of forgiveness. As it says in Job, the price of wisdom is above pearls. Learn from me.

The Merfolk smiled. *I will keep my pearls.* It swam away. But one or two stayed, and perhaps that was enough. I still had a few more minutes before I would run out of air.

The Chat Show Host

"It's the hit wedding of the summer. Now Pulitzer winning reporter Nicola Penbury and her Merfolk spouse Larimar join me for an exclusive interview on the eve of their honeymoon. Nicola, Larimar, welcome!"

"Please, call me Nicky. Thank you for having us. We've brought a sign language interpreter with us so Larimar can speak freely."

Thank you for having me here. Pleased, I.

"I'm delighted to have you! Now, tell me everything! Let's start with your venue. Why did you choose the London Aquarium for your big day?"

It meant a lot to me to be surrounded by teeth-beasts as I would in the ocean. I miss my home so much, and although nothing can really come close to that I love to be at the Aquarium. We have visited many times together and I knew I wanted that to be the place where we would be joined.

"And Nicky, were you scared, diving with sharks?"

"My breath caught at first, but I was soon lost in the moment. It was magical, seeing Larimar there shimmering in the light with sharks swimming all around her. I forgot for a moment that we were in a huge enclosure with guests watching on the other side of the glass."

"The photographs of that moment are very special. And it was the first time we saw your spectacular dress! For anyone who missed it, the designer captured the modern mermaid perfectly. A body-hugging satin sheath down to the calf, then layer upon layer of trailing chiffon mimicking a tail floating in the water. You looked stunning, right down to the white scuba gear! Larimar, what did you think when you saw her?"

I had a waking dream. When we first met many tides ago I thought Nicky's red skirt was a tail of some kind. I did not realise straight away, but she could not breathe. She had fallen from a boat. Heading for shallow water, I, and lucky to have found her. I gave her air and helped her to the surface. I never thought I would see her again. But then they captured me, and she rescued me. That day she wore silver. Our wedding day was the first time I saw her wearing white. The most beautiful creature I have ever seen. Her tail was magnificent.

"And Larimar, you wore the most incredible set of pearls and sea diamonds. Can you tell us about those?"

When war came to my village I decided to flee and give warning to as many as I could. The elders would not leave, but they bid me take the tribe's gems to keep them safe. They were taken from me when they caught me, but Nicky persuaded your army to return them on my release. I had them tied in a traditional style by artist Tomasin. They form a connection between myself and my tribe, even though they are far away, and scattered by bloodshed.

"Did you miss your family at the wedding?"

I will always miss them. I have chosen a life where I cannot return to my clan. I do not know if my family are alive, but they are in my heart and I remember them every day.

"How are you getting on with Nicky's family?"

I think at the start they wanted something different for their daughter. First Merfolk to be seen by the public, I, as a result of Nicky's campaign to free us. It took some time for them to learn to trust me. I don't think they understood my decision to stay female, but Nicky prefers that and they have come to terms with it. We have found respect for each other and I have pride to be part of her family now."

"You said your 'I do's' in sign language. How difficult are you finding it communicating with one another?"

"The only difficulty is in people's expectations that talking should always be with mouths. Signing comes as naturally as speaking when you get used to it. We also speak in touch, and in glances, like all lovers do."

I helped develop sign language for Merfolk in my captivity. I love to find new words and we make our own language together. It is sad sometimes that Nicky cannot understand when I speak, but she is learning to recognise some sounds. It is most funny when she tries to sing.

"Ha, please don't talk about that! Yes, I try to sing along sometimes, I find Merfolk music beautiful."

"Speaking of music, you had a surprise guest at the ceremony! I understand your guests went wild when she joined you in the tank. What did Celtique sing about?"

She sang an old tune, passed down through many families. It gives blessing when two or more Merfolk join together. She sang of peace, unity and love that will last until the ocean is dry.

"That's beautiful. So, your ceremony was presided over by the Church of the Subaquatic, with a special license granted. Nicky, how did it feel to be the first human-Merfolk couple allowed to marry in the United Kingdom?"

"Our campaign to legalise marriage between humans and Merfolk has not been easy. There was a lot of resistance from the public at first, but with more and more mixed couples emerging and sharing their experiences support has slowly grown. When the Bill finally passed in Parliament we celebrated for days."

"So, what comes next for the happy couple?"

"We plan to spend a few weeks together on our honeymoon. We have a specially converted yacht and we will travel the seas together. After that, our work will continue."

There are still thousands of Merfolk stuck in refugee camps like the Sanctuary both here in the United Kingdom and around the world. We will work together to improve their quality of life and to give them basic rights and freedoms enjoyed by humans everywhere. The fight has only just begun.

About the Author

Ida Keogh writes science fiction from her Surrey home, surrounded by cats. Her work has been shortlisted for the Writing the Future Short Story Prize and published in the British Medical Journal and by the Wellcome Trust. In 2021 she won both the BSFA Award for short fiction and the British Fantasy Award for her short story "Infinite Tea in the Demara Café" from the anthology *London Centric* (NewCon Press). She makes sci-fi and fantasy themed jewellery and can be found on Twitter as @silkyida and on Etsy as SilkyfishDesigns.

NP Novellas

2: Worldshifter – Paul Di Filippo
High-octane SF reminiscent of Jack Vance but wholly Di Filippo in its execution. Klom is forced into a desperate chase across the stars, pursued by the most powerful beings in the galaxy, after he stumbles on a secret in the bowels of an antique ship.

3: May Day – Emma Coleman
Orphaned during wartime at just seventeen, May continues with the silly superstitions her mum taught her. Until the one time she doesn't; at which point something dark and deadly arises, and proceeds to invade her life, determined to claim her as its own...

4: Requiem for an Astronaut – Daniel Bennett
30 years ago, astronaut Joan Kaminsky disappeared while testing an experimental craft powered by alien technology. Now, her glowing figure starts to appear in the sky, becoming a focus for anti-tech cults. One man, who knew Joan, determines to find out why.

5: Rose Knot – Kari Sperring
Kari Sperring, historian and award-winning fantasy author, delivers a gripping tale of love, infidelity, loyalty, misguided intentions and the price of nobility, featuring some lesser known members of Arthur's court: the sons of Lot, the Orkney royal family.

6. On Arcturus VII – Eric Brown
Former pilot and planetary pioneer Jonathan James is lured back to the one place he vowed never to return to: Arcturus Seven. A Closed Planet; a world where every plant and animal is hell-bent on killing you; the place that cost him the life of the woman he loved.